SUVI
AND THE
SKY FOLK

Sandra Horn & Muza Ulasowski

Suvi huddled close to her mother as the red sun set.

"Now begins the long dark," whispered her mother.

"Yellow eyes and sharp teeth will come slinking. Keep your ears pricked. Keep your nose twitched. Stay close to the herd."

"Yes mother," said Suvi.

Light from the moon and a scattering of stars shone on the frosty ground. The forest was criss-crossed with shadows. The herd moved out into the open.

Suddenly, silently, shining veils of green and golden and lilac appeared in the sky.

"Oh! Oh! Oh!" shouted Suvi. She began to jump for joy.

"Hush, little Suvi!" her Grand-deer warned.

"It's the Sky-folk! The Two-legs say if you wave or make a noise, they will swoop down and snatch you away, far beyond the stars, where no moss grows."

Suvi shivered, but her mother shook her head.

"That's just an old Two-legs story."

The herd wandered on, now and then scraping for moss under the snow, but Suvi could not stop gazing at the dancing lights in the sky.

Her mother called, but Suvi did not hear.

Suddenly, out of the night came a sound that made the hair on her neck stand up. It was a long howl.

Suvi sprang and ran, bounding this way and that in fright. She could not see the herd. She called out, 'Meh-eh!' but there was no answer. Suvi ran and jumped until she could run no more.

Panting and trembling, Suvi stopped and glanced around.

Nothing moved.

She pricked up her ears.

Silence.

She twitched her nose. The air was empty.

Alone and frightened, Suvi wandered on. She listened and looked, sniffed and called.

Above her, a white bird was perched in a tree, watching her with round amber eyes.

"Who yooo?" the bird called.

"Suvi, a lost reindeer," she answered. "Please, have you seen.....?"

16

The owl blinked, spread her silent wings, and soared away.

She did not care for reindeer. They were too big to eat.

Suvi sighed and walked on. The path began to climb, and the trees thinned out.

Suvi was hungry. She stopped to scrape away the snow. Instead of moss, she uncovered a little furry creature.

"Troll!" squeaked the creature.

"I'm not!" said Suvi. "I'm a reindeer."

"Why did you knock my roof off, then?"

"I didn't mean to," said Suvi. "I'm lost."

Just then the shadow of the owl fell across the snow. The lemming squealed and dived into its burrow.

Suvi was alone again.

Suvi climbed a little higher, and lifted her head to sniff the air. Was there a faint, rank smell? She pricked up her ears.

Was something panting? The hair on her neck stood up.

She gazed fearfully all around. Out of the corner of one eye, she saw something move behind a low rock. It was the tip of a tail, waving to and fro. Sharp ears rose above the rock. Yellow eyes. A toothy mouth.

"All alone?" grinned Old Man Wolf.

Suvi's heart missed a beat.

Old man wolf was very close, and he could run faster than the wind. He did not notice the Sky-folk swirling above. He was too busy gazing at Suvi, waving his tail and licking his chops.

Suddenly, he crouched and sprang.

Suvi screamed and closed her eyes in terror.

There was a soft swooshing noise, and then....

Nothing.

Suvi opened her eyes.

The wolf had disappeared!

She ran for her life,
jumping, bounding, faster
and faster.

"Whoa, little one!" roared
a deep voice.

Suddenly, Suvi was
surrounded by warm coats
and nuzzling noses.

"We've been looking for you everywhere!" said her mother. "We thought you were lost to us! We thought the wolf had got you!"

"He nearly did," panted Suvi, "but he kept waving his tail, and the Sky-folk snatched him!"

"That's just a silly story!" smiled Mother.

"Snuggle up close, little Suvi and don't get lost again."

"I won't!" Suvi murmured.

Old Man Wolf was dazed.

He'd jumped over the rock and
into a deep snow-covered hole.

He shook himself and
clambered out.

High among the stars,
veils of green and lilac and
gold danced.

Down below, Suvi
snuggled close to her
mother.

Old Man Wolf slunk home empty through the snow.

The Northern Lights, or Aurora Borealis, are like dancing veils of colour in the sky, green and gold, violet and sometimes red. They can be seen on dark, clear nights in the skies in countries near the North Pole, such as Canada and the Scandinavian countries. They come from the Sun, which is sending out electronically-charged particles towards the Earth all the time. Sometimes, the Sun sends an extra lot of particles all at once. The particles are attracted to the Earth's magnetic poles, and as they enter the Earth's atmosphere, they glow. That's when we can see them, dancing across the night sky. They are like a special gift to us, and there are many legends about them.

Some Canadian Inuit people believe they are the souls of those who have passed away, and they are enjoying a game of football up in the sky! In Norway, children are told, 'You must not wave or whistle at the lights, or they will come and snatch you away!' It seems a strange thing to believe about something so beautiful, but because they come silently and without warning, people have always thought of them as mysterious, and perhaps a little scary, especially when they glow red. That's the legend I wove into this story

Suvi is the Finnish word for 'summer'. I gave the name to the little reindeer calf in my story because she was born in the summer and she could have been born in Finland, although reindeer live in many northern countries. There are probably reindeer wherever there are the Northern Lights, so I wanted to put them both into a story.

Sandra Horn

The End